A Walk in the Rain with a Brain

EDWARD M. HALLOWELL, M.D.

Illustrations by Bill Mayer

HarperCollins*Publishers*

For Lucy, Jack, and Tucker

A Walk in the Rain with a Brain

Handlettering designed by Daniel Pelavin

Library of Congress Cataloging-in-Publication Data

Hallowell, Edward M.
    A walk in the rain with a brain / Edward M. Hallowell—1st ed.
        p. cm.
    Summary: Lucy meets a brain that helps her realize that everyone is smart
in different ways. Includes a discussion section for parents and teachers.
    ISBN 0-06-000731-1
    [1. Brain—Fiction. 2. Individuality—Fiction] I. Title.

PZ7.H1588Wal2004
[E]—dc21
                                      2002023899

21 SCP 20 19 18 17

One wet day in May
When I went out to play,
I heard near the ground
A gurgling sound.

What I thought was just rain
Was, of all things, a brain!
It looked like a lump of cold smoke.
But then it surprised me
—and spoke!

"Hello, little girl, I'm a brain,
And I'm stuck out here in the rain.
Manfred's my name, for short it's just Fred,
And I fear that I've just lost my head."

"My name is Lucy," was all I could say. He looked so sad, wrinkled, and gray.

"If I don't find my head, Soon I'll be dead," Fred Said.
So we went on a Search for Fred's head.

We talked as we walked.
Soon I asked from my heart,
"Fred, could you please . . .
please make me smart?"

Fred said with a start,
"Everyone's smart!
You just need to find out at what!"

"A long time ago
this was easy to do
Because no one ever made fun of you.

All brains liked to play

And day after day
Each brain found its own special way.

Then a brain named Complain yelled, "Hey, wait!
I am going to create a word for what's best,
So some brains can rule all the rest.
Let's make up a test!"

When the young brains objected,
This one brain infected
The rest with a word they should have rejected.

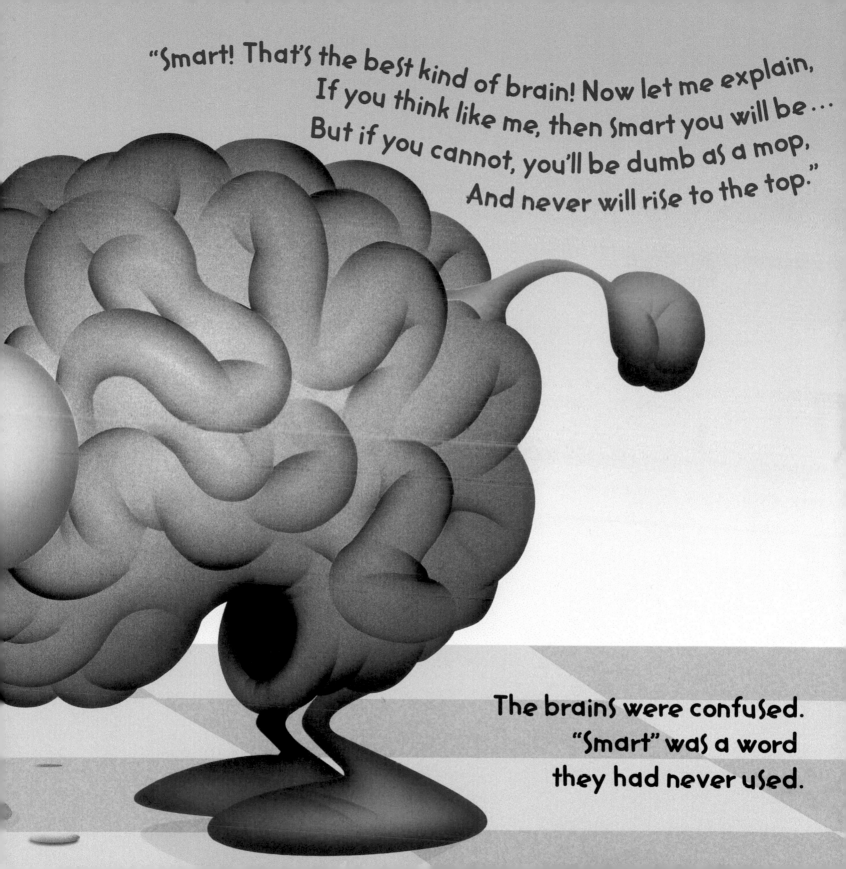

"Smart! That's the best kind of brain! Now let me explain,
If you think like me, then Smart you will be...
But if you cannot, you'll be dumb as a mop,
And never will rise to the top."

The brains were confused.
"Smart" was a word
they had never used.

For years
the brains tried
to make do,
Till one day
a brave brain
named Tru
Told Complain
to go eat
an old shoe.

This makes Complain really mad!

He thinks that play is all bad. Isn't that sad?

"Complain's wrong," said Tru, "I'll explain.
What matters is using your brain.
Yours might make
a new dress—

Or maybe yours
likes to play chess.
Whatever you do
at great length,

Your
brain will
grow there
in strength!"

"So smart doesn't matter?"
Gasped one brain, wide-eyed,
Who usually just tried to hide.

Tru then replied,
"We're all Smart inside.
And no brain Should hide!
What we each need to do,
As we grow, me and you,
Is try all that we possibly can."

"Find something you like,
Like riding a bike,
or bowling a strike,

And have fun with your brain every day.
Brains do best when they play.

Tru then told Complain to stop being a pain.
"Be quiet. Your reign is now ended.
You only pretended that one way was best
So you could be bossy and rule all the rest."

Fred then smiled up at me,
And said, "Thank you
For bringing me home, Lucy.
Remember the words
Of the brain named Tru,
And your brain will help
In all that you do."

I saw my friend Fred dive into his head.
But he said one more time, as he dipped out of sight,
"No brain is the same, no brain is the best,
Each brain finds its own special way."

A Discussion Guide for Parents and Teachers

I originally wrote this story for my three young children. I wanted to teach them a wonderfully liberating truth about the brain: no brain is the best. To thrive, each brain should find its own special way. It is a medical fact that all children's brains have their own particular strengths, ready to develop and grow from the moment of birth, and even earlier than that! But sometimes a strength, or the fragile seed of a strength, doesn't get noticed in school, or at home, or anywhere. When that happens, that potential strength starts to shrivel and disappear.

It is crucial that children do not start believing an insidious myth most people throughout history grew up believing: that only a select few people are "smart."

That belief has held far, far more people back than lack of brainpower ever did. Every brain abounds with the beginnings of talents, skills, attitudes, and enthusiasms that can prove to be useful in life. The art of being a great parent or teacher or coach lies in helping a child identify and develop the best that is in his or her brain.

With proper guidance and encouragement, every child can develop to the fullest the beginnings of the talents and passions that every child is born with. If your child has attention deficit disorder or dyslexia, don't worry. So did Thomas Edison and Albert Einstein. Such children have unusual talents and a special sparkle. With the right guidance, they will shine! Just help them find their brain's special way so they can lead joyful and generative lives. The most common reason that this doesn't happen is that the child never discovers that he or she had any talent that could be developed. The child therefore concludes that he or she is stupid—or maybe just mediocre, or nothing special, or average—and stops looking. For the rest of their lives, these people languish, never having found the passions and skills that should have led them to happy and productive lives.

This book marks my small attempt to plant the truth in the minds of children (and parents and teachers and coaches) before it is too late: All children have magnificent, unique beginnings of talents and passions that they can have fun developing for the rest of their lives. The starting point in finding those talents and passions is play. As children play they find activities they like, activities in which their brains light up. They then practice these activities over and over again, which leads to improvement and mastery. As long as the activity is not purely passive, like watching TV, or numbingly repetitive, like video games, these activities develop confidence and an enthusiastic can-do, want-to-do attitude in life.

After reading the story, I suggest that you explain to your children (or students, or grandchildren, or whomever!) the basics of what brains do. Not all kids know that brains run the show. It's fun—and quite instructive—to help kids make a list of a few of the zillions of activities the brain regulates. For example, your list might include that the brain is responsible for thinking about the story we just read; imagining what happened to Lucy after she said goodbye to Manfred; deciding

what to eat for dinner tonight; telling your muscles to chew; telling you when you are full; waking up; going to sleep; hitting a baseball; learning to spell; thinking up the words you write in a letter to a friend; inventing all that has ever been invented, from the wheel to the computer; feeling happy; feeling sad; figuring out a way to talk your mom into doing what you want her to do; deciding to make up with a friend; and on, and on, and on.

So the brain is very important. You might say, all-important. Now, ask your children or students the following questions:

What does Lucy learn in this story?

What is Manfred, called Fred, telling us all about brains?

As they come up with the answers to these questions, you can let them know that science has proved that "smart" really doesn't mean much. It is like the word, "good." You have to ask, "Smart at what?" or, "Good at what?" Furthermore, you may not think you are smart or good at something that, with a little coaching and practice, you might later become very good at if you allowed yourself to make mistakes at first. Remember, no one learns to ride a bike without falling off a few times, no one can read the first time they pick up a book, and no one hits a baseball without missing it many times.

Next, you can explain to your children that what is most important in developing your brain is using it, and using it to its fullest. You are always using your brain—as long as you are alive—but some activities use much more of your brain than others. Toward the bottom of the list are watching TV, playing video games, or performing unchallenging, repetitive tasks. Right at the top of the list are playing, reading, thinking up new stuff, hitting a baseball, talking and listening, figuring out stuff you didn't know before, making up stories, finding your way when you are lost, putting things together, asking and trying to answer "why" questions, and more!

If you do those kinds of activities, your brain will grow and talents will start to emerge. As often as you can, learn something new. As Manfred said, "That's what we brains just love to do." And play.

As Manfred said, "Have fun with your brain every day. Brains do best when they play." Play involves trying new activities, practicing old ones, and above all, not feeling afraid of making mistakes. In an atmosphere of play, new interests, talents, and skills emerge like seeds germinating in a perfect hothouse.

Next, to help our children pinpoint their interests, potential talents, and developing skills, try asking them the following questions:

What does your brain really like to do?

(All answers are acceptable. The point of this question is to build a long list of activities that your child likes. In that list, you will find the seeds of talents. These seeds will grow if they are properly nurtured.)

What does your brain have a hard time with?

(Again, all answers are good answers. This list will not only help kids identify areas to work on but also make the point that everybody struggles with something and nobody is totally "smart" or good at everything.)

You might at this point ask your children, "How do you take care of your brain?" Brains are powerful, but they do need to be taken care of. After you discuss that question, and probably come up with some strange and remarkable answers, here are some answers you might add:

- Get and give lots of positive human contact. Brains like it when you smile or someone smiles at you. Brains like it when you tell someone you like them or they tell you they like you. It is really important to offer and receive praise as often as you can, every day.

- Ask questions. When you do not understand something, ask for an explanation.

- Never let fear hold you back. The only really dangerous learning disability is fear. If you do feel afraid to ask, then speak to someone else in private, like your teacher or your parent, and they will help you to overcome that fear.

- Find something you love so much that when you do it, you forget who you are or where you are or what time it is. This state of mind was named "flow" by a very wonderful doctor. When we are in flow, we are at our happiest, and our brains are purring. Try to find flow, at least for a few minutes, every day, if you can.

- Look on the bright side. Recent studies have shown that children who are optimistic stand the best chance of becoming happy as adults. And it turns out that optimism can be learned, not just inherited. So, train your brain to look on the bright side.

- Pray or meditate. It calms down your brain.

- Eat a balanced diet. Don't overload with junk food. Your brain lives off of what you eat, so feed it properly.

- Don't use drugs, tobacco, or alcohol. These cloud your brain and can poison it or even kill it.

- Get enough sleep. "Enough" sleep is the amount of sleep it takes for you to wake up without an alarm clock.

- Get lots of physical exercise. Lots of people don't know this, but exercise is really good for your brain. Whenever you exercise you feed your brain in ways that make it better focused, less anxious, and generally happier.

At this point, you and your children are talking advanced neurology! You are discussing what kind of brain you have and how to manage it best. This is a key to a successful, happy life. You have left behind harmful words like "stupid" and "dumb," and you have started on a great adventure of finding your brain's special, best way. It is an adventure that will last a lifetime.